Firebrand Firestorm

The Ancestors of Bjorn Esterday

Volume 15

Holidays

JULY 4, 1776

Wynter Sommers

Published by Pure Force Enterprises, Inc.
California, USA
Since 2002

INGRAM
INGRAM® Distribution

ISBN-13: 978-1-7184-0027-6
ISBN-10: 1-7184-0027-6

DEDICATION

To those who feel strongly about truth,
justice, and the integrity of America;
your honorable actions make us proud.
To those who wonder if their daily
choices matter; your small decisions
impact generations to come.
To those everyday people who don't think
they have what it takes; when you strive
for extraordinary things, the impossible
becomes reality.
Your dreams today become our future
tomorrow.
Thank you for everything you do.

Bjorn Esterday
Was Not Born Yesterday
Series

Firebrand (15 Volumes+Conversation Station Book)
Edges (9 Stories +Conversation Station Book)
Gone (18 Stories + Conversation Station Book)

Bjorn EDGES Series
EDGES Book 1-Swift Encounter
EDGES Book 2-Rousing Attack
EDGES Book 3-One Foot Under
EDGES Book 4-Earthshake
EDGES Book 5-Broken String
EDGES Book 6-Key Witness
EDGES Book 7-Who is She?
EDGES Book 8-Vanish
EDGES Book 9-Chase or Die

Bjorn Series Alternate Reading Plan

1st	Edges Book 1		22nd	Gone Book 10
2nd	Edges Book 2		23rd	Firebrand Vol 9
3rd	Gone Book 1		24rd	Gone Book 11
4th	Firebrand Vol 1		25th	Firebrand Vol 10
5th	Edges Book 3		26th	Gone Book 12
6th	Firebrand Vol 2		27th	Gone Book 13
7th	Gone Book 2		28th	Firebrand Vol 11
8th	Gone Book 3		29th	Gone Book 14
9th	Firebrand Vol 3		30th	Firebrand Vol 12
10th	Gone Book 4		31st	Gone Book 15
11th	Firebrand Vol 4		32nd	Firebrand Vol 13
12th	Gone Book 5		33rd	Gone Book 16
13th	Gone Book 6		34th	Firebrand Vol 14
14th	Edges Book 4		35th	Gone Book 17
15th	Firebrand Vol 5		36th	Firebrand Vol15 (End)
16th	Gone Book 7		37th	Gone Book 18 (End)
17th	Firebrand Vol 6		38th	Edges Book 5
18th	Gone Book 8		39th	Edges Book 6
19th	Firebrand Vol 7		40th	Edges Book 7
20th	Gone Book 9		41st	Edges Book 8
21st	Firebrand Vol 8		42nd	Edges Book 9(End)

ACKNOWLEDGMENTS

We acknowledge those who actively build peace. We acknowledge all the selfless talent which contributed to creating meaningful tokens of consideration and sharing. We acknowledge that every person has a daily choice of right or wrong... and we thank you for choosing the right, good, honorable path filled with integrity because that is the difficult and brave path. Small choices today become lasting monuments of loving hope tomorrow.

CONTENTS

0 PREFACE

When Jane first sought the truth about what really happened to her Uncle Floyd, she did not expect to encounter so many people who together collaborated to help forge a new nation.

She had encountered undue hardships. One of which sent Jane unwillingly to these colonies in the first place. Jane never dwelled on the troubles which befell her. Instead, she focused on the future and appreciated what she did have in the present moment.

Jane's life served as an example of how to live with integrity even if you do not get immediately rewarded. Now... there is a rush to get to the church.

One lesson we learned from last time was that a simple act of consideration ripples into the future. Jane taught Silversmith to read. Jane employed Silversmith, entrusting her with tasks far beyond that of a traditional Lady's Maid. Silversmith used her ingenuity and determination to make the best of what they had and this resulted in an invention which inadvertently preserved Jane's well-being.

Jane's determination to see justice done regarding her Uncle's demise, put Jane in harm's way. Her pursuit revealed the culprit so that such a nefarious individual could no longer hurt others as he had harmed Jane's tiny remnant of a family. Acting with integrity saved Jane on more than one occasion. She took no short-cuts, which tested her endurance, but in the end, she was rewarded with blessings which will cascade to future generations....

1 CHAPTER 151: (JULY 4, 1776)
To the Church on Time

Inside the carriage on the way to the church, Susanna stared at Mrs. Dunlap.

Button Gwinette simply looked on as he rubbed his injured leg.

Eunice gazed out the window.

"Very clever of you to have convinced that sailor to actually drive us to the church, my dear,"

Mrs. Dunlap said to Susanna. "A very efficient use of your charms, I'd say."

Susanna looked away, then announced, "There will never be a good time to confess to you."

"Confess?" Mrs. Dunlap asked as she glanced at Button, "About what, my dear?"

"You must be told before we meet the others," Susanna looked down.

"Is this a matter for just friends?" Eunice, TallMan's mother asked. "Perhaps your confession should wait until after we arrive at the church."

"Told what?" Mrs. Dunlap asked Susanna, ignoring Eunice.

"Jane..." Susanna's throat tightened as she spoke the name of her friend.

Mrs. Dunlap's face brightened, "Yes. Jane will be enthralled when we share this story with her. Oh, I'll have to develop an ocean-themed tea biscuit to serve..."

I don't think she wants to talk about it," Eunice advised Mrs. Dunlap as she saw Susanna's reaction.

"Is this a ladies only conversation?" Button asked. "I should be riding with the other men..."

"Nonsense," Eunice comforted, "You are injured and you are not a footman. You will remain inside the carriage. We are nearly at the church."

"It is impossible to tell Jane," Susanna's eyes started to redden and moisten.

"Why on earth not, Susanna? It's a fascinating set of events!" Mrs. Dunlap retorted, "I don't see any confidences which would be violated by sharing our adventures."

"Because Jane is dead." Susanna blurted out.

"What?" Mrs. Dunlap squinted, as she looked at Susanna, evaluating her,

"Nonsense," Mrs. Dunlap repeated.

Susanna inhaled and then spoke slowly through her quivering voice, "When we rescued Eliza at the docks, she told me that on the ship named The Spy, Eliza saw Mr. Tweedbottom throw Jane overboard at the height of the storm."

"Jane? Our Jane? Into those churning waters? Are you quite certain? It was dark, after all... Of course, Eliza was mistaken. Why, Mr. Tweedbottom would want nothing more than to marry Jane... Eliza's recollection does not make any sense at all. Of course, she was quite mistaken."

2 CHAPTER 152: (JULY 4, 1776) John Adams Mails a Letter and Bjorn Esterday is Named

John Adams walked into the church where the small party were in urgent discussion. "Pastor," John Adams said as he approached the pastor of the small church.

The pastor replied as he hurried to greet the man, "Yes, Mr. Adams? You realize I prayed for you today. How went the meeting at the State House?"

John Adams looked over the pastor's shoulder as he observed the people who were clustered around the front pews. It was Eliza Lucas, Jane, Silversmith, Billy, Polly and her Babe, and of course Magistrate Pinkney with Bryce Aiden Tyler.

"Are you conducting service soon?" Mr. Adams asked apologetically, "I did not intend to interrupt."

"Oh, please do not concern yourself, Mr. Adams," the pastor replied as he turned and explained, "that fellow over here wishes to marry that woman with the blanket wrapped about her shoulders over there. The one who looks the most unkempt."

He turned back to face Mr. Adams, "But what may I do for you?"

Mr. Adams leaned in, "I wrote a letter to my wife yesterday."

"Yes? And would you like to pray the letter is delivered in tact?" the pastor asked.

"Yes. Please," John Adams replied as he gave a brief nod.

Seeing Mr. Adam's response, the pastor asked, "Why do you appear concerned? Is it about this letter?"

John Adams answered, "As I wrote to my wife, Abigail, if the *Declaration of Independence* been made seven months ago, it would have been attended with many great and glorious Events. We might have even been able to possess Canada...."

The pastor looked down sympathetically, "Ah, but the troops suffered from the prevalence of the small Pox."

"True," John Adams agreed, "The seven month delay has emboldened all thirteen colonies to fully embrace and adopt the notion of independence, which will cement our union."

Mr. Adams looked upwards as if considering a new fact, "Actually, the contributions of some of the great minds who actually drafted declarations for their own colonies, such as Virginia..."

Mr. Adams paused to inhale before continuing rapidly, "...and others, contributed to the wording of our united declaration... so I suppose there was no way to rush the creation of such a document, which could establish us as independent from the British crown..."

Before anybody could interject another comment, Mr. Adams continued with confidence. "We could be the first land...the very first, I say... to propose governance of the people and by the people instead of being ruled by a monarch... Imagine... what a fanciful yet innovative concept of justice, equally applied to all... Humph..."

He sighed satisfied, but then added an afterthought, "I suppose we did need that time to craft the language in such a manner that all colonies would agree to sign it, after all."

"Then, what troubles you, Mr. Adams?" the pastor wondered. "Is it the lack of pomp and parade on this day?"

John Adams glanced at the people clustered around the pews near the altar of the church.

He then turned to the Pastor and said, "Future generations should celebrate this great day. Perhaps it should be called the Day of Deliverance by solemn Acts of Devotion to God Almighty."

"That is a rather long name for a holiday," the pastor replied, "What think you of naming it Day of Independence?"

John Adams thought and then said, "I wish I had penned that in my letter to Mrs. Adams. Perhaps I shall propose your idea to her when we next meet."

The pastor suggested, "And if you think it should be celebrated loudly, then there is still time remaining in the day to... to..."

John Adams finished the pastor's thought with, "Games, sport, guns, bells, bonfires and illuminations from one end of this continent to the other?"

Mr. Adams took a breath and glanced upward, as if trying to see the bell tower through the ceiling of the church.

He continued with, "Despite the blood, treasure and toil required to maintain this declaration and defend these states, I see rays of ravishing light and glory! But to formalize such happenings would take a year to plan... the second day of July, when our meeting started, should be the day we remember."

Polly, noticing the pastor speaking with a man near the entrance of the church, handed her babe to Billy Dawes while Silversmith tended to Jane's appearance.

Polly quietly walked toward the Pastor, eager to ask a question, but not wishing to interrupt.

The pastor put a hand on John Adam's shoulder and said a silent prayer. The pastor then looked up brightly and said, "Then, in 1777, we shall formally have all your pomp and loud noises. But today, perhaps I can assist by arranging to have our bells ring out!" He spied a few youths passing by the door of the church and abruptly rushed outside.

The pastor called to the youths and asked, "You there, can you find gunpowder and collect your friends to create cheering and noise in the streets in front of this church? We wish to celebrate an event today."

The youths looked confused.

John Adams tossed a coin at the youths, which made them scramble away to execute the task.

"Thank you, Pastor," John Adams smiled as he turned to leave. "I shall gaze upon your church from afar to witness the pomp and parade you were kind enough to arrange. I shall tell it all to my wife upon my return home."

Polly now reached the pastor and asked, "Pardon me, but may I request a favor?"

John Adams left the church.

The pastor was in a bit of a hurry, "In a moment, my child, as I need to find somebody to ring the bells. Mr. Adams

"requires fanfare to mark the meeting your friends are in."

"But," Polly said as she followed him to one of the side doors and started to climb narrow stairs behind him, "Could you record the name of my son?"

Up the stairs she could hear gunfire in the streets.

"Is this church being attacked?" Polly asked, frightened.

"No! It's the celebration!" The pastor assured, "the one John Adams wanted. It's small and nobody may remember it, but it counts as a celebration." He laughed as he got to the bell and tugged on the lone rope to ring it.

Polly shouted, "I want my son christened in this church, see?"

CLANG went the bell.

The pastor replied shaking his head, "You want one glistened birch... tree?"

CLANG!

The bell rang once more. Shouts were now heard outside. The Pastor leaned over the edge to wave at the youths now encouraging other surprised, but delighted, passersby to celebrate with them in the street below.

The youths even pounded on the doors of the pub and pulled out newly arrived sailors to celebrate and add to the shouting.

Polly persisted and this time shouted, "The church should offer my son a name."

The pastor attempted to repeat what he heard, "You searched wood coffers but guns cause shame?"

CLANG!

The loud bell caused Polly to clap both hands over her ears as she cried, "My son was born yesterday!"

And, then the bells stopped as the Pastor looked at her while the ringing faded for a moment, "Yes, I heard earlier. No need to shout. Your son's name is Bjorn Esterday."

Then he rang the bell again but suddenly seemed to remember something. "Oh! We are having a wedding! I must make haste!"

Dropping the rope to clang the bell, the pastor rushed down the tiny steps. Polly, surprised at his sudden movement, tried to follow after him.

All Polly could manage to say was, "No..." In an attempt to clarify the matter.

However, he responded, distracted, with quite another subject. "The new soprano should sing for the couple. I must fetch her."

While flying down the staircase, he stopped suddenly and turned to Polly, who was above him on the narrow steep stairs trying to keep pace with him.

The pastor instructed, "You join the others in the pews while I ready everybody for the ceremony, my child." He resumed scampering downstairs.

Then he stopped again, turned back and ordered, "Oh! That bell must keep ringing. Today must be celebrated! You saw how I did it. Could you ring those bells while I get prepared for the most rapidly paced wedding I have ever performed?"

He picked up the corner of a hanging wall tapestry and then turned back to Polly and bit his lip saying, "Oh, I do hope it will be acceptable. And, your son's name shall be recorded."

Then, without another word, the pastor disappeared behind that tapestry, which apparently was concealing another passage.

Feeling helpless standing there on the tiny steep bell tower stone staircase, Polly shrugged.

3 CHAPTER 153: (JULY 4, 1776) The Scribe's Carriage Arrives

Patrick Scriobhai's voice could be heard shouting, "Whoa" to slow down the horses which pulled Mrs. Dunlap's carriage.

He could be heard by the silent party inside the carriage.

The pealing of the bells, which Polly was now ringing, reverberated around the streets. The youths in the streets were making merry and encouraging Patrick, who was halting the horses, to come down and join them.

He shook his head at the youths with a smile. "Those bells are so loud!" Mrs. Dunlap commented.

"Perhaps," Eunice suggested, "...it is the start of the hour."

TallMan offered, "Or perhaps a service is about to commence?"

Inside the carriage, Mrs. Dunlap stared at Susanna Wright as did Eunice and Button. The horses slowed to a stop in front of the church.

As Patrick Scriobhai secured the reins, TallMan bounded out of the seat and hit the ground with a thud. Then TallMan began helping the passengers to descend from the carriage.

The party gazed on at the closed church doors until every person alighted from the carriage among the cheers and laughter of the slowly growing crowds in the street just in front of the church.

Susanna looked up at the bell tower, and remarked, "The bells do sound festive."

Patrick approached Susanna, "Would you like to wait outside with me? Join the street party?"

Ahead of them, some youths were piling small mounds of gunpowder on the streets, placing a string, then lighting it and running away with mischievous shouts until it exploded. Then they would cheer and repeat the process.

Susanna shook her head, "No, but you should join us inside the church, Patrick, as I will need to pray for my sin of omission."

"You'll have to tell somebody, you know... Jane's..." Mrs. Dunlap whispered to Susanna implying Polly or Silversmith, but not wanting to say names. She tried to be heard over the noise.

Susanna nodded, "I don't think anybody would be able to absorb such bad news. Perhaps after, we might go back to the docks to collect Eliza and she can speak of it directly."

Mrs. Dunlap shook her head, uncertain that waiting was the best course of action to inform Polly that Jane had died at sea.

"Well, we must tell both the good and bad news plainly. Just the facts," Mrs. Dunlap affirmed as she pulled up her skirts a good three inches above her ankles to permit her feet more freedom to march up the stairs with alacrity.

Susanna bounded in front of Mrs. Dunlap, then faced her, turning her back to the church doors. With pain lacing her words, she grasped the hand of Mrs. Dunlap and pleaded, "I cannot tell Silversmith. I cannot."

For a long moment, Mrs. Dunlap looked Susanna in the eye. TallMan and Eunice watched both women silently.

The bells continued to ring out.

Patrick, uncertain about his place with these people, remained hesitant to climb the stairs to the church and, instead, opted to be a steady support for the wounded Button Gwinette.

Mrs. Dunlap looked firmly at Susanna, then glanced over Susanna's shoulder. The church door was not closed all the way, as it had appeared earlier. It was open a crack. A stream of dusty light distinguished one person who stood inside at the front of the alter.

Mrs. Dunlap's laughter escaped her throat, "Ridiculous my dear, Susanna." She continued to walk, "I assure you, Silversmith will greet the news of Jane just as I feel at this very moment."

"I don't understand," Susanna replied in a harsh whisper, "This makes no sense to me. Why are you not as crestfallen as I?"

Pulling open the door, Mrs. Dunlap

directed Susanna gently to look inside the church. Mrs. Dunlap asked, "Who do you see at the front of the church... the alter, there? In the light... Standing next to that Bryce fellow? You know he came to my house looking for Jane..."

Susanna slowly turned around and saw Silversmith, smoothing out Jane's hair as best she could.

Susanna replied softly to herself, "And that Bryce fellow found her." Then running into the church, Susanna cried, "Jane?"

The name echoed and ricocheted against the walls of the nearly empty sanctuary. Jane turned around and, suddenly smiling, cried out, "Susanna!".

Susanna rushed to her grasping both of Jane's hands in her own, overcome by emotion, "You are alive!"

"Barely!" Jane replied, "It is indeed a very long story..."

Both the women laughed.

Susanna froze.

She had thought her friend Jane Hargreaves was dead, yet here she stood before them in this church.

Susanna then saw Eliza Lucas and gasped, "Eliza! I thought we would need to collect you at the docks!"

"Magistrate Pinkney, here," Eliza exclaimed, "found both Mr. Tyler and Jane and brought us all to the State Building in hopes of meeting up with all of you, but we saw Polly and Silversmith on the street in front of the church and decided to wait for you, here."

A sunbeam of light illuminated Jane as Silversmith used the light to repair Jane's disheveled appearance as best she could.

Jane, holding the large ring Bryce had given her earlier, too large for a finger, too small for a bracelet, suddenly saw

Mrs. Dunlap. Jane struggled against the pain of her wounds to turn toward Mrs. Dunlap. She required the steadying aid of Silversmith.

"That spare skirt I loaned you, Miss Susanna," Silversmith started, "I'm so glad you brought it with you in the carriage, as Miss Jane's skirts were tattered... It suits her, does it not?"

Jane added as she rustled her skirts, "Silversmith made a pannier out of cork. I'll share the whole story with you later." She clutched the rough blanket around her shoulders to cover up her torn bodice.

TallMan and Eunice were just entering the church, careful not to interrupt the joyfully noisy reunion. Jane smiled at Mrs. Dunlap, "Is the meeting over? Did you get it signed?"

Mrs. Dunlap proudly showed the copy she held, "Not all signatures, but enough to start the most infectious enthusiasm for being a free country!" She smiled proudly, "There may be some alterations, but my husband, Mr. Dunlap, will get those broadsides to be approved before this day is out."

Then, Mrs. Dunlap paused and looked at the large candle-ring Jane grasped. She saw the others standing up: Billy Dawes, Silversmith, Eliza Lucas, and Magistrate Karl Pinkney.

Mrs. Dunlap and Susanna were both perplexed and they both asked at the same time, "What is afoot, here?"

Patrick was helping Button up the stairs of the church and had just reached the entrance, but all eyes were on Jane and Bryce.

4 CHAPTER 154: (JULY 4, 1776) The Surprise Wedding Guests

Inside the church, facing the altar stood Mrs. Dunlap, Susanna Wright, TallMan, Eunice, Eliza Lucas, Magistrate Pinkney, Silversmith, and Billy Dawes holding Polly's baby. They created a crescent around the happy couple about to be wed, Jane Hargreaves and Bryce Aiden Tyler.

Mrs. Dunlap looked around and asked, "Where is Polly?"

"Oh, yes!" The pastor said as he rushed to his big dusty records book and opened it. "She wanted to help keep the day in a celebratory mood, so she is in the bell tower ringing the bells, as I requested." He dipped his quill into the inkwell and penned something in his book.

Then, the Pastor asked Bryce, "I have noted Miss Hargreaves' name and the date. May I have the spelling of your name, sir?"

Bryce spelled his name.

Mrs. Dunlap looked at Susanna Wright and asked, "What is transpiring before my eyes?"

Jane replied, "Mr. Tyler has asked me to marry him... this very day. We waited for the meeting to be dismissed so that you could join in our celebration!"

Bryce added, "We can have a proper ceremony later, but I want to share the story of this loving union with our future children and the memory must include all our friends."

"Oh! I am so pleased!" Mrs. Dunlap replied, "Oh! This is a splendid day of achievements all around."

Susanna added, "My friend, whom I feared was dead, is wonderfully alive! The Magistrate has shown great kindness by bringing Eliza and Bryce Aiden Tyler and Jane to us here... And now a wedding!"

Then the pastor acted as if he had just suddenly remembered something, "Oh! I must fetch our Soprano!" His eyes darted to all the spaces where one may enter the corridors behind the main sanctuary and then made his selection laughing to himself, "So difficult to choose an entrance." He picked a doorway and bustled to it, turning around and calling out to the crowd, "I shall return shortly with your music."

Mrs. Dunlap hurried to the pastor to ask discretely, "But Polly should attend the ceremony. Could we not ask her to stop ringing the bells and join us?"

The pastor paused a moment, then thoughtfully said, "Yes. Yes. Certainly! I shall send her down presently. But we must make merry." And, abruptly, he vanished behind a small door.

Mrs. Dunlap looked around. "Where is that new fellow, Patrick?"

Susanna added, "Oh, I believe he is helping Button Gwinette navigate that entrance." Indeed when the small party looked to the entrance, they saw the two hobbling forward.

Mrs. Dunlap charged to the front entrance of the church, walking with such speed, she nearly slipped on the polished stone floors.

"What is taking so long?" she demanded as she approached the entrance. She noticed Patrick and

Button were now talking with others from outside in the growing crowd.

Patrick replied, "Oh, these youths were paid by some fellow to make merry and they've coincidentally gathered up my blokes who were waiting for me in the pub."

Each of the men gave a slightly inebriated but polite nod to Mrs. Dunlap. Button turned and smiled, "They are all quite pleasant fellows."

Mrs. Dunlap shook her head, "You boys," she instructed the youths, "Continue to make merry as you have been instructed, but I require the men to join me inside!"

She looked at Patrick and said, "Bring all your friends inside. We may as well have more wedding guests."

Patrick turned to his mariner companions and announced, "Inside, you watery souls, as we shall be witness to a wedding!"

With drunken cheers, they all tumbled into the church, fighting for shoulder breadth through the tiny doorway inside the larger door.

"You can enter through the larger door as it is ajar," Button suggested. Then he looked at Mrs. Dunlap and added, "I think I'll sit on these steps and wait out here. I do not think I could witness a wedding. "

Mrs. Dunlap opened the larger church door wide to allow the sailors easy entrance.

Then she saw Button Gwinette preparing to sit down, favoring his injured leg. Mrs. Dunlap rushed to him, grasping his biceps and aiding him to a standing position once more.

As Mrs. Dunlap clutched Button's arm she said, "It is quite necessary for you to be inside, my good man."

She started to walk him in behind the other sailors. As they entered the church,

Mrs. Dunlap saw a shadowy alcove and helped Button to lean against the carved out space. Then she went back to fetch his walking stick and handed it to him.

Button replied, "Oh, I am quite winded. I don't think I can walk any further." He looked pleadingly into Mrs. Dunlap's eyes, "Please, I can't have the others see me cry over my memories which can never be shared with my beloved."

Mrs. Dunlap replied, "Now you rest here, lean against the wall or sit on the floor, if you like. They can't see you cry from back here in the shadows. But, you must promise me, Mr. Gwinette, that you will remain for the entire wedding ceremony. "

Then they noticed the bells had ceased to ring. Smiling, Mrs. Dunlap added, "Promise me!" "Aye," Button Gwinette said, "I'll remain, as you wish."

Satisfied, Mrs. Dunlap hurried to catch up with Patrick, who was now introducing his sailor friends to the rest of the party near the altar of the church.

Eliza mentioned to Jane, "Oh, I wish I could have brought a gift to celebrate your wedding."

Susanna shared, "Jane! You wanted to ring in the new year of 1777 in a new gown. Well, you don't need Mr. Tweedbottom for that! In six months we can create for you a splendid gown."

Eliza Lucas also smiled and agreed, "Yes, Jane. With Susanna's silks and my indigo blue... You do realize the indigo cakes I make, hold their value and could be considered a type of gold to trade for other goods... a blue version of gold..."

She smiled impishly as she continued, "Blue gold....while paper currency seems so unreliable... It would be delightful to have a dress made of blue... something blue... it would be symbolic of the enduring value of honor which forged the union of our thirteen colonies, which will be a new stronger nation. This new union could impact the world, as your union will impact generations to come... think of something blue..."

Susanna finished the sentence, "We can create a gorgeous gown in the color of Azure blue skies." Then she looked at Bryce, "And we can make you a matching waist coat in the same fabric! Consider that a wedding present to both of you... but you need only wait a few months for Eliza and me to create it."

Mrs. Dunlap said in despair, "Oh, I don't know what I could offer as a wedding present."

"You needn't offer anything," Jane smiled. "That you are all here celebrating with me right now is more than enough."

"I know," Mrs. Dunlap quickly added in a whisper so that Button could not hear, "what Polly would give you."

"Bacoun?" Silversmith and Billy said in unison.

"No, no, no." Mrs. Dunlap laughed, "Her husband had given her vellum to pen their love story to share with their child, remember?"

Silversmith added, "Oh, I remember getting it repaired." Billy interjected, "At the shoppe I suggested."

Jane cautiously asked, "A thoughtful sentiment, but would she really want to pen something on that vellum other than her own love story?"

"She already has," Mrs. Dunlap explained. "So, she couldn't give it to you if she wanted to," Mrs. Dunlap leaned in to loudly whisper, "Polly used her husband's vellum to pen this copy of The Declaration, which has already been signed with many of the necessary signatures... and I still need to get broadsides back to John Hancock before the day is out!" Mrs. Dunlap added, "When is the ceremony going to begin? I have broadsides to deliver!"

5 CHAPTER 155: (JULY 4, 1776) Still in the Church

Patrick and his sailor friends took a seat in the pews, pulling Susanna Wright to sit next to them. Patrick made certain to sit between Susanna and the rest of his drunken sea faring friends.

Susanna leaned forward to where Eliza Lucas and Magistrate Pinkney had decided to sit in the pew in front of them.

Susanna asked, "The bells have stopped tolling, so does that mean Polly will join us and we can begin the ceremony?"

Eliza turned around, careful not to hit Magistrate Karl Pinkney, and whispered, "I think we still need the Pastor and his Soprano."

Mrs. Dunlap overheard and added, "And Polly, too. I'm sure she's on her way down from the bell tower."

All at once, the door near the altar was opened, and Polly emerged.

She smiled at her friends and hurried to find a seat next to Mrs. Dunlap. Billy Dawes, sitting on the other end pointed to the baby bundle in his arms.

Polly nodded.

Billy handed the cooing baby boy to Silversmith, who handed it to one of Patrick's sailor friends, who handed it to TallMan, who handed it to Eunice, who handed it to Magistrate Pinkney, who handed it to Eliza Lucas, who handed it to Mrs. Dunlap and finally to Polly at the opposite end.

While this occurred, a door close to the entrance of the church, near the alcove in which Button Gwinette was standing, opened. From the perspective of those sitting in the pews near the alter, the door opening was obscured by the strong late afternoon sun. Long shadows of street crowds danced along the walls of the sanctuary.

Above all the street noise, the party at the front of the church, near the altar, could hear the thud of a door being forced and a man falling.

"Oh! Did the pastor fall?" Jane, worried, whispered hoarsely to Bryce.

"I don't know. I'll investigate." Bryce was about to walk down away from the altar, where he was standing with Jane, along the aisle toward the church entrance, when out of the shadows, emerged three forms.

One on each side, with an injured hopping man in the center.

Mrs. Dunlap squeezed Polly's hand. Polly was entranced by her baby and not paying much mind to the happenings around her.

6 CHAPTER 156: (JULY 4, 1776)
Walking Down the Aisle

Eunice asked, "Who is over there? Is that the Pastor walking toward us?"

Most of the small party turned to look at the shadowy figures, which emerged from an alcove, now approaching them.

At first, with the sun blinding those seated in the pews of the church, they could not discern shape or size, but then the silhouette of individuals started to take form.

Magistrate Pinkney commented, "There are three of them. Did the pastor say he had one or two sopranos?"

Eliza offered, "These churches have a network of passages behind the sanctuary. It is no wonder the clergy seem to appear from nowhere."

Susanna added, "I didn't know there was a door down there."

Slowly the flanked injured man hopped, grunting slightly with each step he took. His walking stick was clumsily and ineffectually tapping the floor in front of him.

Those on either side supporting the limping man, the pastor on one side, and a woman on the other, were guiding this fellow by looking down at his feet to synchronize their steps with each other. Those flanking him guided the injured man closer to the altar.

As they approached, the seated party could hear the pastor apologizing, "I am so sorry for shoving that door opened. I had no idea you were on the other side and that I would cause you further injury to what you have already incurred."

The man in the center, obviously trying to silently suffer through the pain he was feeling, simply clung to the shoulders of his two aids, the pastor and this woman, and smiled as he grunted with a shot of pain searing into his bones with each hop he took.

Feeling guilty, the pastor added, "I am remiss for my haste has caused me to render you harm." He leaned over to the woman and asked, "Can you not sing a soothing lullaby which would remind him of his mother tending to his wounds when he was a boy?"

The woman nodded and as they approached ever closer to the altar; the sounds from the rambunctious youths celebrating in the streets seemed to attract even more crowds and the noise level outside rose.

A moment's pause was followed by the woman's voice singing,

"O Waly, Waly up the bank.

Farewell, farewell, all hope of bliss.

For Polly always must be thine..."

Then, Polly broke free from the group, the only person to approach the trio.

Silversmith rushed to Polly to take the babe from her arms. Polly did not even look at Silversmith and kept her gaze locked onto the three approaching figures, now coming into light.

Instinctively, the others somehow knew Polly needed time.

The party paused.

Some stood and some remained seated. They all watched as Polly slowly stepped toward the three.

Polly suddenly became aware of very mundane things, such as the realization that she was approaching them on the balls of her feet, as if careful to not dispel a dreamy cloud.

Cautiously, Polly took another step. Gingerly, the trio approached as Button hopped on one foot, now holding the walking stick.

The party did not make a single sound.

Barely audible, Polly uttered to herself, "I prayed and did not believe a miracle could come to pass. Yet I fear even now, I am dreaming," With tears in her eyes and dry mouth, she asked the approaching trio, "How can this be?"

7 CHAPTER 157: (JULY 4, 1776) Surprise Wedding Guests

Jane clutched the large ring Bryce had given her earlier as she realized what must be happening.

Mrs. Dunlap held her breath. Susanna and Eliza looked on with amazement.

The men in the party seemed to miss the current of electricity, which had just shot through Polly, causing her to forget the babe in her arms, had it not been for

Silversmith who rushed to Polly to take the child.

Silversmith, bouncing Polly's cooing baby in her arms, took a step closer to Billy Dawes, who now rose from the pews.

Dumbfounded, Polly stared at the trio approaching the alter with their eyes downcast to guide the wounded man's steps... an elderly woman on one side, the pastor on the other.

Polly shook her head, as if she was awaking from a dream, and said, "...you should reward a constant heart since alas 'tis so seldom found..."

"Oh, you skipped a part from the Beggar's Opera," the elderly woman instinctively corrected while still observing the good hopping foot of Button Gwinette.

"Mama?" Polly asked cautiously.

Now the elderly woman slowly looked up as she realized the voice was familiar.

Before responding, she evaluated Polly very carefully.

Mrs. Dunlap stood up and sandwiched herself to sit between Eunice and TallMan.

She clasped both their hands, and then releasing that of TallMan, produced a handkerchief from the wrist of her sleeve and poised the lace-trimmed cloth to dab her tears, should they emerge.

All looked on with compassion as they witnessed this reunion. Polly asked again, more softly, "mama?"

The elderly woman attempted to speak, yet nary a sound escaped from her lips. She took a deep breath to calm her rapidly beating heart and then found her voice and said, "*A stóirín?*"

Polly could not move, could not speak, shaking her head in disbelief as to what her eyes were actually witnessing.

Polly's mother, Mrs. Mulhoolin's, voice cracked as she whispered, "My little love... my bonnie Polly?"

Polly, now saw the face of the injured man in the middle. Slowly he looked up and his eyes met Polly's.

Polly gasped and took a step backwards.

"Polly?" the limping man asked in a soft, barely audible voice.

Gasping, Polly's eyes welled up with tears as she clarified, "Button? But, the raid..."

"I'm alive..." he managed to whisper. "And... you are, as well..."

Polly, now thawing from her frozen moment of disbelief, rushed to Button, throwing her arms around him, sobbing, "I had given up hope. I am so sorry, my Button. I had come to terms with your death, but you are here. You are really here..."

He inhaled Polly's scent, now satisfied he was embracing his very own wife once more, after their unbearably long and painful separation. His hand cradled the back of her head as he felt the familiar softness of her hair. Button huskily whispered in her ear, "Polly, we must never be apart again."

Polly, riddled with conflicting emotions started to apologize, "Oh, Button. The vellum you bought to pen our love story, I... I... I had used that to pen the Independence document... I am so... "

Button pulled the sobbing apologetic Polly to him, crushing her in his embrace.

Tears started to roll down Button's face as he struggled for breath to speak words of comfort to his wife, "...Our vellum will be the foundation of freedom for all Colonists. You have taken our love story and turned it into a love story between the colonies and their new country. Well done, Polly. Well done."

The pastor stepped away, touched by this unexpected reunion, but the woman standing beside Button did not move.

Polly now, breaking free from Button's embrace took a step backward and smiled with a tiny laugh, *"Mamai*...This is Button... my husband... and father of our son..."

Silversmith quickly approached with the baby bundle she was entrusted with, and held out her arms for Polly to take the infant to present to Polly's mother.

Silversmith whispered to the pastor, "My! Is this Miss Polly's very own mother reunited after such a long separation?"

The pastor nodded with a smile, "God works many wonders for the noble of heart."

Polly's mother, Mrs. Mulhoolin, accepted the cooing baby in her arms, transfixed by his innocent gaze. She bravely attempted to stoically refrain from tears, yet the cascade of emotion rained tears of joy like a waterfall.

Polly and Button both engulfed the older woman in their embrace, and caressed her with tender soft words of comfort.

All of them stood, hugging and crying, awkwardly uncertain about how to proceed.

There was no socially acceptable etiquette instructing the proper protocol for reuniting with loved ones you thought were lost forever.

Polly's mother smiled up at Button, and then looked at Polly with an old familiar glance, which mothers give to their children to remind them to behave properly.

Mrs. Mulhoolin asked Polly, "An Englishman?"

"Oh, he is very different, *Mamaí*, I assure you," Polly explained

"Then," Mrs. Mulhoolin inhaled slowly and nodded, "I welcome you, son, to our family."

Button Gwinette smiled and bowed as best he could while trying to balance on one good leg. "I thank you for your indulgence, Mrs. Mulhoolin, and for the rare gift of such a wonderful daughter who agreed to become my wife." Button smiled broadly at Polly.

Polly continued, "I cannot believe you are here, Mama..." as she showed her little boy's face to both Button and her mother, "and that you are now a grandmother."

Mrs. Mulhoolin, Polly's mother, replied, "Oh, my bonnie lass, *A stóirín*, I told you I'd find a way through the church, God be willing. When an opportunity for passage to the Colonies presented itself, I took it."

With tears welling up in her eyes, she forced herself to breathe as the joy of being reunited with family beamed from her like a comforting ray of sunny hope, which had pierced through the dark cloud of impossibility.

Family. Love. Together. Longing satisfied. All past troubles now forgotten as this moment of reunification proved to be so very worth the sacrifices to get here.

8 CHAPTER 158: (JULY 4, 1776)
Names and Couples

Mrs. Dunlap stood in the center aisle of the church and announced, "I want to remind everybody that I have the location where John Hancock is residing this night. I am thrilled to be witness to this, but I do need to make haste to retrieve the new broadsides from Mr. Dunlap's print shop and return them to Mr. Hancock for approval."

Billy Dawes leaned over and assured Mrs. Dunlap, "I have the fastest steeds on my carriage and they are rested, now. After this, I'll get you to your husband's print shop and back here before the morrow, Mrs. Dunlap. Don't you fret."

Satisfied, Mrs. Dunlap took a seat in the pew facing the alter, "I'll remain silent, then."

Polly turned brightly to her mother and said, "Yes! The friend who rescued me from certain death is about to be wed."

Polly held her little boy closely in one arm, while she took Button's hand, helping him hop to a nearby pew as the tiny family sat close to each other.

Her mother moved toward the pastor.

Button, now seated in the pew, looked over at the babe in Polly's arms.

The infant bundle cooed, as he looked on lovingly into the child's eyes. "I cannot believe this is our child. He is so healthy and happy." Button gazed at Polly, as he touched the baby's small hand. "He is so very tiny. What did you name him?"

Then as Polly's mother, Mrs. Mulhoolin, walked to her place near the alter to sing for the wedding, the Pastor instructed Jane where to stand to exchange her wedding vows with Bryce.

Button leaned over to TallMan who sat nearby and said, "'Twas hired Indians who ripped me from my wife. 'Twas you, sir, who united us and made certain my baby was safe. I would like to make an alliance. An alliance not just between you and me, Sir, but between my future generations and yours..."

"Done!" TallMan said as they clasped forearms, "You can honor this by asking your future generations to name their first born the name of your son."

Button leaned back smiling, "As soon as we decide on a name..."

9 CHAPTER 159: (JULY 4, 1776)
Sailors Request & Blessings

Inside the church, the Pastor looked to one of the sailors and asked, "Would you mind ringing the bells once the ceremony ends? We want it to be very festive."

The sailor stood up smartly, saluting the Pastor as if he were a sea captain. Realizing the level of inebriation this sailor was experiencing, the Pastor added, "Or perhaps you could be in charge of cheering after vows are exchanged."

The sailor replied, "My mates are able to embrace this duty of ringing the bells with hearty gusto!" All the other sailors agreed and cheered enthusiastically eager to embrace this duty.

Eunice leaned toward Button and said, "Mr. Gwinette, I thank you for this gesture of alliance. This honors the very tribe, which adopted and raised me."

Button nodded with, "We have all suffered our own tragedies as we strive for a better tomorrow."

Eunice added, "God used the ripping away from my English birth family to become a bridge between the people native to this land and the Europeans seeking asylum from tyrannical monarchies. The kindness of my adopted family proved to heal many wounds."

Polly looked at her own newly born son.

Eunice leaned over to Polly, now cradling her newborn. Eunice touched the baby's hand. The tiny fingers wrapped around Eunice's thumb.

Eunice declared, "I, on this day, bless your son with God's grace. May your newborn child learn to heal the wounds of many peoples with the skill to negotiate peace, fight for justice, and always embrace learning to achieve many goals." She paused smiling at the wakeful babe, who cooed at all the adult faces surrounding him.

"Thank you so much," Polly whispered gently.

Button chocked back emotion as he added, "If God can reunite me with my wife and guide the formation of our new country, then I only hope all future generations will possess the honor, integrity, and ingenuity to be worthy of the blessings you've bestowed upon my son...and this new and precious land." He nodded with appreciation to both TallMan and Eunice.

The Pastor approached the pulpit and chortled to himself as he announced, "I can see that many more of you will need to have me perform nuptial ceremonies." He pointed at Eliza Lucas and Magistrate Karl Pinkney and said, "You two."

Then, the pastor's fingers indicated Silversmith and Billy Dawes, "And you two."

Finally, he located Susanna Wright and the Sailor Patrick Scriobhai, "And I see you two... all of you will be very happy together in the very near future!"

Enjoying the fact that he had just made everybody there quite flustered by pointing out the emotions of love, which they all had tried to repress, the pastor continued, "Now, I believe we are here to wed this lovely Jane Hargreaves and Bryce Aiden Tyler."

The Pastor looked around, "Are there any other requests before we begin?"

Jane turned to Bryce, smiled, then to

the Pastor and said, "I have a request..."

Curious, the Pastor motioned for Jane to elaborate.

Jane walked to Mrs. Mulhoolin near the alter, and took her by the hand, guiding her to the pew in which Polly and Button sat.

Jane said, "When I started on my journey, I wanted to find the truth about how my Uncle Floyd had died. During my journey, I met a wonderful friend in you, Polly."

Jane smiled, then turned to Button as she continued, "I had hoped that by completing the mission my uncle had started, which was to halt the widespread practice of kidnappings for the nefarious purpose of enslavement for profit, that I could help Polly resolve the loneliness and loss she felt when she thought you, Button, had died. Mrs. Dunlap confided in me that she tried every one of her husband's printing connections to find some communication about what might have happened to you, Button, but she was at a loss."

Mrs. Dunlap added, "But in my quest, I met TallMan and his mother Eunice. Friends for life, I'd say." Mrs. Dunlap nodded appreciatively at TallMan and Eunice.

Jane concurred and continued by addressing Polly's mother, "But, you, Mrs. Mulhoolin... Although Polly missed you, nobody could ascertain how to reach you."

Jane took a breath, "God opened doors at just the right times. Now that you have found that you are a grandmother, I am certain you will want to be close to your daughter, Polly."

"That I would, but I've just arrived and need to..." Mrs. Mulhoolin started.

"Please," Jane interrupted, "Allow me..."

Bryce quickly added, "And permit me to help you all stay together as a family, just as your lives brought Jane and me together."

Jane turned toward Bryce and smiled lovingly, then addressed her lady's maid, "Silversmith?"

"Yes, Miss Jane?" Silversmith stood up.

10 CHAPTER 160: (JULY 4, 1776)
Silversmith's New Earth Farmers

Inside the church, and right before her ceremony, Jane was about to ask Silversmith to take on a new duty.

Jane looked over at Silversmith and said, "Now that Mr. Tyler and I will soon be family, would you, Silversmith, embrace the task of finding a home for Polly, her husband and child along with some manner of accommodations for Mrs. Mulhoolin?"

"Oh! Yes, Miss!" Silversmith excitedly added, "I know Witherspoon." She looked at Polly and Mrs. Mulhoolin and explained, "That's Miss Jane's uncle's butler", then Silversmith continued, "Witherspoon mentioned a cottage for let near the grand estate back home." Then she recalled another fact and added quickly, "The barn with the secret meeting. The one the red coats invaded. There is a large vacant building near that barn. The barn where Miss Susanna Wright and Mr. Button Gwinette partook in the secret meeting. That is another option for Mrs. Mulhoolin."

Billy Dawes thoughtfully added, "An abandoned building could serve as a cloister after we clean and furnish it. Perhaps Mr. Tyler could consider acquiring it."

"A cloister?" Mrs. Mulhoolin replied, "Just for widows? Oh, perhaps I might find other women who could join me in that cloister." She crinkled her nose adding with a nod, "It would be comforting to have like-minded company."

Silversmith added, "And with the knowledge that TallMan and his mother possess, I'm sure they could teach you how to tend the earth to make it yield all manner of fruits and vegetables."

Eunice looked at Jane and asked, "Is this cloister open to all widows?" Jane replied, "Yes. You are now considered family... you and TallMan."

Eunice looked up at TallMan, "After we return to Canada, I wish to introduce you to somebody who, I suspect, will help you forget your loss of love and may make you never wish to leave the tribe, save for a visit to friends... or to take me to this new widow's cloister."

TallMan blushed.

Mrs. Dunlap asked, "Must one be a widow to visit? Or to learn to farm the earth?"

Jane Hargreaves looked at Mrs. Dunlap, "I want to have a place where all travelers, near and far, rested and weary can consider themselves welcomed. Silversmith is quite clever and I'm sure she can organize such lofty undertakings."

Silversmith suggested, "I do have some knowledge of gardens and such. I could help you learn what I know and then perhaps if we can get other widows to join you, we can all teach them to be earth farmers, as well..."

Jane clasped her hands, "Oh, Silversmith, that is divine. You are now in charge of the earth farmer knowledge sharing mission..."

Silversmith beamed, "I'll do a very good job with this new mission teaching how to cook what you grow... and with your permission, Miss Jane, my gift to you shall be teaching your little ones... when they come... the joy of cooking and inventing."

Jane smiled as her eyes welled up with tears at such thoughtfulness, "That would be a gift, not just to me and Mr.

Tyler, but to our future generations. Thank you, Silversmith. Sharing your talents is a splendid wedding gift."

"Miss Jane?" Billy asked awkwardly. "Yes Mr. Dawes?" Jane replied.

"Well, if I can enlist Miss Susanna's help to foster a connection with Benjamin Franklin, I think I could help improve the roads so that it would be easy to get to and from the cloister... and deliver goods and letters to and fro or whatever might be needed to develop this earth farmer concept."

Polly caught Jane's eye and softly spoke, "Thank you so much for helping me keep my family together." Jane nodded understandingly.

The pastor interjected, "It won't be just about farming, but about living in accordance to God's will and spreading hope in an untamed land fraught with battles and chaos. I would be happy to visit and help, if that would be welcomed."

Eunice shook her head, "Amazing how strife, kidnapping and slavery has affected each one of us... the residents of these colonies..."

The pastor sharply replied, "Oh, do not think the Bible supports those concepts. Nay! In the Bible, the term 'slave' is better translated as salaried servant, sometimes in a managerial post, for a period of a decade or less and definitely not past their late thirties, as some scholars claim was the case in first century Rome. However, here, today, in our still British colony, some traders indulge in atrocities, such as kidnapping and slavery for life."

Eunice asked, "Where in the Bible are such practices condemned?"

The pastor replied, "First book of Timothy. First chapter, verse nine through eleven." He paused then thumbed through the old testament of his Bible and said, "Oh! And Deuteronomy chapter twenty-four, verse seven. Oh, yes. I must suggest Leviticus twenty-five, verse ten be used in a speech a fellow is writing."

"What is the significance of that verse?" Eunice asked.

The pastor thought a moment and then recited as he flipped through the Old Testament of his Bible, "...Proclaim liberty throughout all the land unto all the inhabitants thereof: it shall be a jubilee unto you; and ye shall return every man unto his possession, and ye shall return every man unto his family"

"Oh, that's a good one to remember. We should have that carved and mounted someplace," Silversmith suggested.

"It already is... or a portion of it," The Pastor explained, "I know of it because it is inscribed on our bells. Tomorrow a fellow trained by Whitechapel Foundry, the place which makes all the best bells in England, is to take down all our bells in Philadelphia to polish them...or was it to be the fellows of Pass and Stow?" The pastor shook is head and continued, "The inscription was first ordered on a bell for the State House in 1752 and two years later, a similar bell was ordered for Christ's Church in 1754. They are both so similar in style... I do hope the fellow and his cleaning men won't get the two mixed up when he remounts the bells."

TallMan added, "These atrocities and injustices you alluded to earlier are the very reason so many meetings occurred. Much discussion was required to develop this Declaration of... of... ?"

Jane nodded as she finished the sentence, "...of Independence. Yes, TallMan... it is." She smiled at the pastor and said, "Pastor, I think your visits would be most welcomed." Then she happily regarded her assembled wedding guests. "All of you must visit us."

Jane Hargreaves then returned to Bryce, taking his hand and using the ring to keep her blanket taught around her shoulders so she could hold both his hands.

"Well, I think," Jane leaned over to Bryce, "this wedding day is perfect. Simply perfect! I could not have planned anything better..."

Bryce Aiden Tyler replied softly, "God works in very mysterious and sometimes slow ways. I would not normally thank God for trouble and strife, but in our case, my love, without it, we would not have such a joyous moment as this."

Jane whispered, "Splendid. Thank you, Pastor, for your promise to visit us. That was my only other request." Jane turned to face all those who sat in the pews to witness the impromptu wedding, "...to join all our skills to make each other's lives better." She gazed into Bryce's eyes, "Let us celebrate the day of so many miracles..."

"And future plans," Mrs. Dunlap added.

The Pastor stretched out his hands

and said, "Glad we resolved these issues. I realize we are not in the bride's home and we are here in the heat of summer. Unusual for a wedding, but 'tis a fitting day to celebrate!"

He opened his Bible and prayer book. As he flipped through the pages, the pastor said, "Now, beloved friends of Miss Hargreaves and Mr. Tyler, we are all here today to serve as witness to joining these two souls in holy matrimony. From this day henceforth, God shall bless and guide you both as husband and wife in your life together..."

He looked down at his prayer book and said, "Oh, here it is..." he found the proper page and started to read it with formal solemn tones.

He occasionally paused as the street crowds outside became noisier, making merry, just beyond the church entrance.

11 CHAPTER 161: (JULY 4, 1776) Just After the Wedding

Jane giggled as she adjusted the large ring Bryce had given her, which held bits of the blanket around her shoulders. She grasped Bryce's hand, now feeling a bit dizzy. Her heart started to race as she realized this moment was changing her life from this day forward.

The pastor smiled at the two being wed,

Jane and Bryce, and then beamed at those sitting in the pews witnessing the ceremony of holy matrimony.

"You are now, husband and wife!" The pastor declared.

Every person in the audience stood and applauded, shouting, "Mr. and Mrs. Tyler! Mr.and Mrs. Tyler".

When the ceremony was completed, the sailors surrounded Jane and Bryce in a ring by holding hands with each other while the couple was encircled therein.

As the others joined in the circle, their entire wedding party marched the couple, still enclosed in a ring of wedding guests, outside the church into the street festivities.

All at once, five sailors broke free and raced each other back inside the sanctuary, slipping on the polished floor as they skidded to a halt at the tiny door leading up to the bell tower staircase.

Laughing and mimicking bells, themselves, these jolly fellows pushed each other, single file, up the staircase.

"That pastor asked ME to ring the bells," one stated as he grabbed for the rope.

"Nay we all signed up for the clang-the-bell voyage," another said as he also reached for the bell.

Then another leaned over the other two and grabbed for the rope, but the force of his body flung the two previous bell ringers out onto the rope and they all became lofted up into the air as the bell rang and then they all landed at once while the other two stood with arms akimbo, laughing at the site.

The two stationary sailors grabbed the remaining ropes and rang them with furious jubilation. "We got the big bell!" the three guffawed.

"I am fine with the small bell," snorted another after he hiccuped.

The fifth raced to the church balcony edge and leaned over to yell at people in the streets. As they looked up, he shouted, "I spy another seafaring mariner!" He leaned over and shouted, "Oi! Oi! Ye, there!"

Sailors in the street looked up and shouted back, "Get to the State House and ring the bells there as hard as you can! Follow us!" These sailors waved and raced in the direction of the State House.

Moments later nearly every bell in the city was ringing, bursting with joy and merriment. The fifth man jumped onto the rope with the three other sailors. All were laughing uncontrollably as they tugged at the rope, unable to hear each other yelling.

With the weight of the forth, the large bell clapped so hard that it sounded a bit dull.

The fourth sailor, who was ringing the smaller bell, stopped. The bell still rang out as he abandoned his rope to join the other four at the big bell.

They all stepped back... and let it swing to a stop naturally. One whispered harshly, "You cracked it."

"I did not!" protested the sailor. "That thing is over a ton. I'd wager... two thousand pounds."

"It's got a small crack!" the responsible fourth sailor, who had manned the small bell, pointed out.

The fifth sailor retorted, as bells from the state house could be heard everywhere. "The Pastor said they'd be cleaned tomorrow, so no harm. They'll get fixed."

"We've got to let the pastor know... his bell won't ring the same," the responsible fourth sailor answered, hands on his hips.

"I'm not telling him," the first sailor protested. "This Copper pot isn't supposed to crack. Look at it! It's nearly a dozen feet around."

The second sailor offered, "Well, if it's a small crack, it can't get any bigger, let's keep ringing and tell the pastor later! Besides, that bell polisher will fix it in the morning. That's what they do, isn't it?"

And two of them kept ringing the bell, "Sounds just as good as before..." they tried to convince themselves.

Two sailors raced down the stairs calling behind them, "Meet us at the State House..." Those remaining in the bell tower tried to ignore them, then suddenly scampered after them.

As they raced out the door, the first sailor stopped and grabbed the pastor saying, "Pastor! We rang the bell! Might have a wee bit of a... scratch... some might call it a crack... Thought you might want to tell your Whitechapel bell cleaners... We'll be at the State House ringing their bells."

"Thank you, sailor," the surprised pastor replied, "I'll be sure to tell him to polish it up..."

Off they raced down the street, fighting the thick crowds all cheering and making merry.

12 CHAPTER 162: (JULY 4, 1776)
Throwing the Rice

Eliza reached into her skirt pocket as she smiled and glanced at the couple still surrounded by laughing wedding guests in the thick of the crowd.

Eliza then turned to Magistrate Karl Pinkney, "I do not have confetti, but I still have some rice seeds in this tiny container. It holds the rice from my father's plantation in South Carolina. Would it be inappropriate to toss it at the newly married couple?"

Magistrate Pinkney nodded his head and reassuringly added, "I think this day, we can start new traditions. Throw the rice! I predict it will become this nation's number one exported crop. You will be bestowing wealth and blessings on the happy couple."

With a grin, Eliza tossed her one handful of rice at the couple.

Dogs eagerly clustered around the church to sniff the rice and look for other treats dropped by the crowds.

Birds fluttered with excitement around the couple, occasionally snatching a grain here and there.

Eliza squeezed Magistrate Karl Pinkney's hand and said, "You shall have the finest indigo blue coat and we shall all ring in the New Year in a regal blue manner. You, Susanna, Jane, and I will even make something for Silversmith and all our new beaus."

Patrick the sailor, having overheard, leaned into Eliza and Karl Pinkney and said, "I think a new year's celebration as you describe could convince me and my blokes to become land lubbers for a while. We like the people, here in these Colonies..." Then he pushed off to find Susanna in the crowd.

Outside, the youths had emptied the pub and all the immediate homes and places of business. The crowds were cheering, as John Adams had wanted earlier.

Mrs. Dunlap grabbed Billy Dawes and Silversmith and they headed straight for the carriage so that she could return quickly holding the Document adjustments, which John Hancock needed to approve.

With the growing crowds, it was clear celebrations would last far beyond when Billy Dawes would return Mrs. Dunlap with those broadsides, at which point everyone could join in the party.

The pastor followed the wedding party with Mrs. Mulhoolin and paused at the front door of the church. "July 4th 1776 shall be a memorable day indeed, Mrs. Mulhoolin." The pastor sighed, "I'm pleased Mr.Adams' wish for celebration coincided with this wedding."

"Indeed, Pastor," Mrs. Mulhoolin smiled as she looked at huge crowds of people in the streets making merry. Then, she turned to the pastor, "But my new grandson. We need to record his name, do we not?"

"Oh! I've done that," the pastor grinned as he glanced at his old records book, "along with that couple who just married... and I made note of the names of the other couples, who I suspect will marry in the very, very near future." He smiled at Mrs. Mulhoolin, "I'm so glad you arrived safely. I am going to enjoy... our... professional," he cleared his throat and continued, "relationship..."

Mrs. Mulhoolin looked away, a slight pink shaded her alabaster cheeks and her lips coyly smiled. Then she became very matter of fact and asked plainly, "But, the babe hasn't been named..." Mrs. Mulhoolin protested, "He was born yesterday."

"That's right," the pastor replied as his eyes gazed upon the effervescent happy masses celebrating in the streets, "I've recorded his official name in my book as Bjorn Esterday."

The bells rang out and the streets were filled with crowds of celebrants, singing and shouting their joy at the day.

※ **THE END** ※

13 What Just Happened?

You have completed the story of early American Firebrands from the 1770's who are the ancestors of the characters in the EDGES and GONE series, which starts in the 2030's .

To find out how they are related, please see the DESCENDANTS section of this book.

In this saga, we witnessed how the characters suffered undue hardships in order to help others and uncover the truth. It was difficult to fight the established royal system to selflessly forge a new way of governing by collaboration and cooperation in these

Colonies. It was challenging to overcome the obstacles of communication, travel, and ideals to get the representation of each colony to agree that they should unite and eventually declare their independence from the crown and form into a united nation of states.

Even the smallest of choices made by each of the characters forged a path which led to another decision. The character and integrity of each individual dictated whether the next step on their journey would be for the better or for the worse. Trying to "short-cut" and make selfish decisions, not only had consequences for one's own life, but also for the lives around each individual. And continuing to be influential were the lives and choices of those who came before them, their ancestors.

Those who made difficult, risky, but morally sound decisions, laid the secure foundation of their future, which impacted their descendants for many generations, opening doors of opportunity.

After reading this story, do you think the choices you make today matter?

Do you consider the consequences of even the tiniest selections you make?

Does your heart and soul confirm that your true motivations are stemming from honor, integrity, truth, justice, and morality?

Do you evaluate the decisions made by people around you, and are you able to judge if those choices impact others for better or for worse? How does your level of respect change when you observe a pattern of choices made by another? Do you think their true hearts are revealed by what they choose?

Do you ever consider that your decision today could influence a future generation?

In this final volume of Firebrand, we saw the necessity to quickly arrive at the little church. We saw how the name for a new babe was selected and a new tradition initiated. In this story, the first born son will be given the name Bjorn. In the decade of the 2030's, when EDGES takes place, we meet a descendant also named Bjorn. We discover how he takes everyday circumstances or challenges and endeavors to make honorable choices as did his ancestors during the 1770's.

So the generational tradition of naming a son also taught honor and integrity to each generation, which resulted in making their society and community a better place in which to live.

What traditions would you want to start which may impact the future of your children or future generations?

In this story, John Adams confirms, in a letter he wrote, the actual date of Independence for these Colonies, a feat nobody thought could ever occur; an event which defied doubts and exceeded expectations, but also required all residents to agree to help each other to cooperate and defend freedom so they could be stronger, united together, as a new nation. With freedom comes responsibility to maintain that freedom.

In this story, we also witnessed a joyful unexpected wedding. Jubilant sailors were invited to be guests to celebrate the moment of nuptials, which coincided with the formation of a new country, a nation of united colonies which soon evolve into united states...of America.

They were free to respect their neighbors, free to abide by the same set of laws which applied equally to each citizen regardless of their social standing and class.

They were free to create and innovate, free to grow and develop.

What does freedom mean to you?

Have you considered what is important about a milestone ceremony such as a wedding? What other memorable events in your life should be acknowledged with a ceremony?

Is it the superficial appearance of merriment and levity?

Or is it the demonstration of how a union can be welcomed and cemented by participants in attendance?

Witnessing the judicious union of colonies as well as witnessing the union of an honorable, wise, hard-working, intelligent, and noble man and woman in matrimony are both landmark occasions which could forever alter, and in most cases bless, future generations.

What choices will you make to create a better world for everyone?

14 Did You Know...

In an earlier volume of Firebrand, a reference was made to the document *Reflections on Courtship and Marriage.* The text, penned in the 18th century, is replicated in this section. This will give you insight into how personal letters became an underground commentary on the institution of marriage. Many sought this document for advice regarding romantic relationships.

This text uses some archaic words, phrases and spellings, which have been left in tact to provide insight into the marital advice given in the mid 18th century.

Although this work was published by "B. Franklin", which we assume is Benjamin Franklin, some say that it was in fact curated by Mrs. Elizabeth Timothy, a Dutch publisher. At that time, certain topics could not be published by a lady, and therefore some suspect that her original comments were actually published by Mr. Franklin, a friend of her family.

The replicated text includes archaic spellings, grammar and punctuation.

Not all archaic words have been defined and may require an etymological dictionary.

This document is referenced in a discussion between Silversmith, Billy Dawes and Mr. Peter Timothy, the son of Elizabeth Timothy in the book: **Firebrand, Volume 7, Continuous Chapter, titled *"(JUNE 1776) In the Meeting Town Bookshop"*.**

Reflections On Courtship and Marriage:

IN TWO LETTERS TO A FRIEND.

Wherein a Practicable PLAN is laid down for OBTAINING and SECURING CONJUGAL FELICITY.

Philadelphia:

Printed and Sold by B. Franklin, 1746.

By the late 1740s, many documents on courtship and marriage were being written from a desire to clear away social confusions of the past, to reclaim adults and youth alienated by social writers who had failed to recognize the advent of the Age of Reason.

Increased attention was given to the talents and intellectual capacities of women ; discussions of religious aspects of romantic and marital love were supplemented with an assessment of related social values and concerns. The anonymous Reflections on Courtship and

Marriage deliberately attempts greater fairness and less chauvinism than what is exhibited in writings from earlier periods—and is partially successful. Its author deplores the fact, for example , that the education of women is generally "extended no farther than to superficial and exterior Accomplishments"; that "their Behaviour is rather owing to a Sort of mechanical Influence, than to Sentiments from Reason and Judgment."

A marriage formed on such passion and superficiality, says the author, can not last. After such a couple are married, "and have taken their Full of Love," the "young Spark's Rant" ends, and he finds that "Passions are extreamly transient and unsteady, and Love, with no other Support, will ever be short liv'd and fleeting."

Like many of his contemporaries, the author of "Reflections" argued that, through certain "excesses," even a married couple became guilty of informal immorality. In addition to private restraint, the author called for public discretion between marriage partners.

It is in his discussion of marital roles that the anonymous author is most alienated from modern sensibilities, most obviously chauvinistic in his contentions. He begins well enough, opining that marriage "is a certain voluntary and mutual Contract between the Sexes, the End or Design of which is, or should be, their joint Happiness."

But in asserting that there are times

when the husband or wife alone must take control, must guide the family, the author falls back on male-centered tradition , declaring, "Really, Nature and the Circumstances of human Life, seem to design for Man that Superiority, and to invest him with a directing Power in the more difficult and important Affairs of Life."

Although the writer is careful to point out that the truly wise man - the "Man of Sense and Breeding" - will never abruptly wrest such authority from his wife, the writer clearly makes the woman man's subordinate, suggesting that much of the responsibility for keeping the marriage in tact - and keeping the husband virtuous - belongs to the wife.

"To a Man of any Delicacy ,and even moderate Neatness," he proclaims, "nothing certainly is more odious and ungrateful, than a slatternly and uncleanly Woman; 'Tis enough to quell his strongest Passions, and damp every fond and tender Emotion ."

The woman who exhibits "Negligence and Dirtiness of Person" taxes her husband "with the Want of his Senses, with the Taste and Appetite of a Hog, whose Joy is Filth." Predictably, the writer says nothing about the responsibilities of the husband to groom himself for his wife, or to otherwise make himself attractive to her. He mentions only that "no ridiculous Vanity or foolish Ambition should suffer the Husband or Wife in their Dress, Furniture, or whole Way of Life, to exceed their Income or Fortune"; and that "their Appearance and Expenses, should neither degenerate in to Sordidness, nor run into a wild Extravagance."

Reflections on Courtship and Marriage was a popular and influential text in its day, and remains the closest thing we have to an eighteenth century American marriage manual.

Despite its frequently dated observations, the text is always engaging, often witty, and occasionally very wise indeed .

from the ADVERTISEMENT

The Author of the following Reflections, endeavors to lay a practicable Plan, by the Execution of which, the matrimonial State may produce such a Crop of Felicity, as to make it highly worthy the Pursuit of every reasonable and virtuous Mind. Had he wrote for publick View, he would probably have appeared in a more full and regular Dress, - but that has already been apologized for.

We shall only therefore declare our Opinion, that his Plan carries Reason and Conviction with it; and might perhaps more fully have done so, had he considered his Subject by Way of Contrast, as forcibly as he has in the Abstract.

For whoever has observed the declining Days of Old Batchelors in general, may see their unconnected, unrelative State in Society, tottering to their Graves in a gloomy Solitude, or, at best, only attended by a few artful rapacious Vultures, who impatiently wait for their Prey. No tender affectionate Companion, of similar Mind and Manners, whose constant Sunshine of Love, warm'd the Spring and Summer of his Days, and now with an unalterable Friendship and Fellow-feeling, accompanies him Arm-in-Arm thro' the dreary Wilds of his Winter, with the Guard of a Son or Sons, whose filial Piety and manly Vigour, is ever ready to protect him from the insolence of others, or to defend him from those Calamities to which our feeble Age exposes us; surrounded with a prattling Offspring fondly caressing their hoary Grandsire, and blooming a Prospect of future Honour and Virtue. . . But these divine Supports are as little to be expected by an Old Batchelor, as in our Power to describe.

Our Author's Reflections may furthermore convince the Fair Sex, that tho' Fortune may buy them a mercenary

Tyrant; tho' Beauty may provoke their Ruin, or attract some Fop or Cox comb; yet, Good Sense, and real Merit only, will touch the Heart of, and maintain their Influence over, Men of true Worth and Knowledge: That the Charms of Judgment, Discretion and good Temper, are the only lasting foundations upon which matrimonial Felicity can be built; That the Cultivation of their Minds is absolutely necessary to the Production of their Happiness; that Love will soon Starve without Friendship; and finally, that as the Standard of human Felicity in government is the PRACTICE OF WISDOM AND VIRTUE; so also of the Conjugal Union in marriage.

from REFLECTIONS

ON COURTSHIP and MARRIAGE

IT is alleged, on the one Hand, that the Education of Women, in general, must naturally give them a strong Bias to Dissembling and Affectation, the Turn of Thinking, which, for the most Part, they early imbibe; the too much Attention, and Artifice they are taught to bestow on their Persons; the trifling, arid often ill-judged

Accomplishments, by which their Ambition is excited, and in which, for the most Part, they so studiously endeavour to excel.

BY this Method of Management they are polished to a superficial Lustre, dazzle our Sight, and work up our Passions. But, for that End, the substantial Culture of their Minds is grossly neglected; true good Sense, and sound Judgment; the inestimable Perfections of a generous, an open, and noble Mind, are but little considered in their Educations.

HEREBY are they quite unfitted for the delicate Pleasures of a rational Esteem, and the God-like Joys of a manly Friendship.

NOT having therefore the requisite Fund of substantial Worth to raise the Thought, and touch the Heart; to be an agreeable Companion, and a steady Friend; and only striking the Springs of Passion and Appetite; when those are deaden'd, as they naturally will be by Possession, the joys of Wedlock grow dull and insipid, sicken and die away, leaving us in their Room, a vain and capricious, an empty *and insignificant Companion, with perhaps a helpless Infant or two, to increase our Care and Vexation.*

. . .

The common Education of Young Ladies is chiefly extended no farther than to superficial and exterior Accomplishments; and their Behaviour is rather owing to a Sort of mechanical Influence, than to Sentiments from Reason and Judgment; Reading and Reflection are too much neglected by them, or ill regulated; their Taste of real Worth and Merit in Men and Things, is thereby render'd very defective, and often shows itself to be mighty ridiculous; their Passions are rather kept under Restraint by the common Rules of Decorum, than by any rational Conviction of a real Beautiful, [or of the] deformed in Character, independent of who sees, or who knows. . .

They aim more to catch the Eyes, than penetrate the Heart, to blow up the Passions, than to secure the Understandings of their Admirers; Esteem and Friendship are more remote from their Attention, than frothy Compliments and foppish Rant.

. . .

I am persuaded no one in this Company will assert, Women are by Nature constituted incapable of Friendship, or any social Charms which our Sex possesses. Every Person here is better versed in History and human Nature.

WHAT then should obstruct their shining in so exalted a Light? - Why, Education. . . Allowing what we have said on the Education of Young Ladies to be all true; do not our Sex too often compleat what that sex has begun: do we not in general flatter them with a Heap of bombast Stuff, and then laugh at them for seeming pleased with it? Do we not blow up their Vanity and Conceit, with Notions of that Merit to which they have no just Title? And gloss over their silly Airs and Follies with false Applause, and Epithets of Approbation? Do we not generally converse with them in a Language of Rodomontade and Nonsense? . . .

HOW then, is it possible for them to improve; How to discern real from false Excellence, who seldom hear a Word of Sense, and less of Truth? 'Tis this Sort of Treatment Young Ladies meet with in common Life, and too much of this Kind we carry with us when we make our matrimonial Addresses; to which, and our subsequent Imprudences after Marriage, I cannot but ascribe them any just Satires that are thrown out against it.

. . . [I therefore assert the following:]

THAT unhappy Matches are often occasioned by mere mercenary Views in one or both of the Parties; or by the head strong Motives of ill conducted Passion.

THAT by a prudent and judicious Proceeding, in our Addresses to a Young Lady of a good natural Temper, a probable Foundation may be laid for making her an agreeable Companion, a steady Friend, and a good Wife.

AND that after Marriage, by continuing in the Road of Prudence and Judgment, we may erect a Super-structure of as much real Felicity, and as refined an Enjoyment of Life, to its latest Period, as any other Scheme can justly lay claim to.

WHAT abominable Prostitutions of Persons and Minds are daily to be seen in many of our Marriages! How little a Share has real Friendship and Esteem in most of them!

How many play the Harlot, for a good Settlement, under the legal Title of a Wife! And how many the Stallion, to repair a broken Fortune, or to gain one! ...

THE real Felicity of Marriage does undoubtedly consist in a Union of Minds, and a Sympathy of Affections; in a mutual Esteem and Friendship for each other in the highest Degree possible.

But in that Alliance, where Interest and Fortune only is considered, those refined and tender Sentiments are neither felt nor known.

. . .

Unhappy Marriages are often occasioned from the Headstrong Motives of ungoverned Passion.

THE cool and considerate Views of Interest, have taken so deep a Root even in very young Minds, that those feverish Marriages are not very common ; and we are, I think, nowadays, more liable to them in our Dotage than our Bloom.

AN amorous Complexion, a lively Imagination, and a generous Temper, are so apt to be charm'd with an agreeable Person, the insinuating Accomplishment of Musick and Dancing, unbon Grace, and a Gaietè de Coeur, that it is instantly transported, sighs, languishes, dies for Possession.

IN this distempered Condition, and Valorous Fit of Madness, his [the lover's] sanguine and heated Imagination points her [the loved one] out to him, in all the romantick Lights of an Arcadian Princess, an Angel Form, and a heavenly Mind, the Pride of Nature, and the Joy of Man, a Source of immortal Pleasures, Raptures that will never satiate, Bliss uninterrupted, and Transports too big for Expression.

Bloated with all these nonsensical Ideas or Chimeras, worked up to a raging Fit of Enthusiasm, he falls down and worships this Idol of his own intoxicated Brain, runs to her, talks Fustian and Tragedy by wholesale. Miss blushes, looks down, admires his Eloquence, pities the dying Swain, catches the Infection, and consents, if Papa and Mamma will give theirs.

THE old People strike the Bargain; the Young Ones are made light-headed with those ravishing Scenes their warm Constitutions and distempered Fancies present to their View.

WELL, they are married, and have taken their Full of Love. The Young Spark's Rant is over, he finds his imaginary Goddess mere Flesh and Blood, with the Addition of a vain, affected silly Girl; and when his Theatrical Dress is off, she finds he was a lying, hot-brain'd Coxcomb.

THUS come to their Senses, and the Mask thrown off, they look at one another like utter Strangers, and Persons just come out of a Trance; he finds by Experience he fell in Love with his own Ideas, and she with her own Vanity.

Thus pluck'd from the soaring Heights of their warm and irregular Passions, they are vext at, and ashamed of them selves first, and heartily hate each other afterwards.

From hence arise Reproaches, Contradictions, &c. Thus all their fantastick Bliss ends in Shame and Repentance.

IN serious Truth how can it be other wise?

PASSIONS are extreamly transient and unsteady, and Love, with no other Support, will ever be short liv'd and fleeting. 'Tis a Fire that is soon extinguished, and where there is no solid Esteem and well cemented Friendship to blow it up, it rarely lights again, but from some accidental Impulses, by no Means to be depended on; which a Contrariety of Tempers, the Fatalities of Sickness, or the Frowns of Fortune, may, for ever, prevent, as Age most certainly will. . .

LET us, on the contrary, proceed with Deliberation and Circumspection.

Let Reason and Thought be summoned before we engage in the Courtship of a Lady.

. . .

IN our Addresses, let our Conduct be sincere, our Tempers undisguised; let us use no Artifices to cover or conceal our natural Frailties and Imperfections; but be outwardly, what we really are within, and appear such as we design steadfastly to continue.

. . .

FOR my own Part, I woul'd, if any thing, be rather less careful and exact in my personal Appearance, before than after Marriage, because the Difficulty of raising an affection, is not so great, as that of preserving it; as every little personal

Embellishment may be serviceable in the former Case, so it undoubtedly will in the latter. - But the Care of our Persons, tho' 'tis seldom neglected before, yet 'tis often so notoriously after Marriage, that I believe many unhappy Ones are caused by it. . .

LET our Manner of conversing with a Mistress be void of fulsome Flattery, and the ridiculous Bombast of Novels and Romances.

LET us my Friend, on the contrary, use her wedesign for a Wife and Companion, to the Conversations of sober Reason and good Sense:

Endeavour by every probable Method, to inspire her with the Sentiments of a rational Esteem, a generous and steadfast Friendship for us.

. . .

NOTHING in Nature is, I think, more odious and contemptible than a female Pedant, a formal, a conceited and affected Wit; whose Brain is loaded with a Heap of undigested Stuff, and is eternally throwing up her confused Nonsense, in hard Words ill pronounced, jumbled Quotations misapplied, and a Jargon of Common-Places; in order to let you know she is a Woman of Reading; whereby she convinces you, she has taken a great deal of Pains to render herself a Fool of the first Class, and of the most irreclaimable Kind.

THE Barking of a Lap-dog is not more grating to the Ear, than the Gibberish of their impertinent Clacks; and the Chatter of a Parrot infinitely more entertaining. In short, such Women are the Mountebanks of their own, the Dread and Contempt of our Sex.

BUT must these jingling Pretenders to Wit and Sense, exclude us from the delightful Harmony, the amiable Conversation of a modest and unaffected Fair One, in whom a good Understanding is joined with a good Mind?

HOW engaging are the Graces of such a Character! How insinuating are its Charms! How imperceptibly does it win over the Mind! What a Flow of tender Sentiments, it diffuses thro' the Heart! Calms each rougher Passion, and swells the Breast with those exquisite Emotions that rise above all Description. . . .

. . .

Where there is any Similitude of Minds, Sentiments of Friendship will beget Friendship.

LET us then take every Opportunity of testifying our Esteem and Friendship: Court the Understanding, the Principles of Thought, and conciliate them to our own.

HEREBY we shall as it were enter into the Soul, and take Possession of all its Powers; this should be the Ground-work of Love, this will be a vital Principal to that, and make our Concord as lasting as our Minds are unchangeable.

Children should undoubtedly be extremely tender in thwarting the Wills of their Parents: Should be very careful, that their Passions do not blind, or their Caprice mislead them: Should with great Calmness and Impartiality reason with themselves: Appeal to their Parents, with great Deference and Humility: Consult with some wise and unbiased Friend: Desire their Interposition.

In short, do every Thing in their Power to convince and persuade; and nothing but a manifest and conscious Violation of Reason and their real Happiness, should force them to oppose or disobey the Will of their Parents.

. . .

Prerogative and Dominion in Marriage, are often Matters of Dispute in Conversations; but more frequently the Causes of Animosity and Uneasiness to the Parties themselves.

. . .

MARRIAGE, in my Sense of it, is a certain voluntary and mutual Contract between the Sexes, the End or Design of which is, or should be, their joint Happiness.

'TIS therefore absurd and ridiculous to suppose or conclude, that either Party do thereby consent or bind themselves over to an imperious or tyrannical Sway .

IT follows therefore that Marriage, does neither by the Laws of Nature or Reason, give either Party a tyrannic and arbitrary Power over the other; and that the Exercise of such a Power , is contrary to the Will and Happiness of any rational Being; and must in consequence render a matrimonial Life uncomfortable and miserable.

REALLY Nature and the Circumstances of human Life, seem to design for Man that Superiority, and to invest him with a directing power in the more difficult and important Affairs of Life.

A Man of Sense and Breeding, will be as it were superior, without seeming to know it; and support his Influence with so great a Delicacy, that his Wife shall ever seem to be his Equal, make use of a thousand polite Methods even to elevate her Character. What an amiable and engaging Scene must such a Couple exhibit!

How firm their Union! And how harmonious their Lives!

. . .

AMONGST those who have a real Esteem and Friendship for one another, there will, strictly speaking, be no Separation of Pleasures: For tho' one Party does not actually share in the other's Pleasure; yet they will in Effect do it by the Force of Benevolence, and be pleased, because the other is so, whether they relish the particular Cause or not.

IN such Pleasures as 'tis proper and prudent for both to share, they should, I think, endeavour to unite their Tastes.

THE more unexceptionably that People in a married Life make the Pleasures of One become the Pleasures of Both, the more uniform and complete will their joint Happiness be.

MODESTY and Decency in our Conduct and Persons, both in Publick and in Private, should most strictly be observed.

. . .

THERE is a certain Purity and Decorum to be preserved in our most retired Pleasures. 'Tis no extraordinary Paradox, that a Man may himself debauch his own Wife; and a Woman harlotize with her own Husband.

But this Subject must be touched with great Nicety; therefore, I shall only add, that even our most unobserved Behaviour, should carry with it such a Spirit of Refinement, as to prevent that vulgar and libidinous Degeneracy, which will infallibly blunt the Edge of our Joys, and in the End pall our Relish.

WE should likewise behave with a modest Delicacy in public.

IN the really well -bred Part of the World, a great Elegancy, and a polished Neatness of Conduct, in married people towards each other, is inviolably preserved. Nothing is a more evident Mark of a rustick and coarse Education, than a Want of this Discernment and polite Carriage.

ALL frothy Tendernesses and amorous Boilings-over, are Insults on and Affronts to Company. What Entertainment is our Love, and are our Passions, to People who do not feel the one, nor are to gratify the other? What a preposterous Regale are our Dalliances to such?

TIS surprising, tho' but too common to see (amongst both Sexes) many, who before Marriage were very assiduous, in the Adorning and Neatness of their Persons, that afterwards grow negligent and highly culpable by the Reverse:

Which Inattention and Remissness, I verily believe, is often one of the first and most effectual Methods to cool the Affections, and estrange the Hearts of many a Couple.

And herein, according to the most impartial Observations I have made, the Ladies are most blameable.

...

TO a Man of any Delicacy, and even moderate Neatness, nothing certainly is more odious and ungrateful, than a slatternly and uncleanly Woman: 'Tis enough to quell his strongest Passions, and damp every fond and tender Emotion: 'T is vastly more so in a Wife, than a Stranger, for as to mere Person, the keenness of inclination is (I suppose) generally less after than before full Possession.

Therefore a slovenly and unfragrant One, in a Wife, must naturally run a great Risque of weakening, if not extinguishing,

Desire. Besides 'tis an Insult upon a Man's Taste, an Affront to his Senses, and bullying him to his Nose.

THIS Negligence and Dirtiness of Person (if we expect or desire a Man to love us at the same Time), is taxing him with the Want of his Senses, with the Taste and Appetite of a Hog, whose Joy is Filth .

LET us survey the Morning Dress of some Women.

DOWN the Stairs they come, pulling up their ungarter'd, dirty Stockings —

Slip-shod, with naked Heels peeping out — No Stays or other decent Conveniency, but all Flip Flop —

A Sort of Cloth thrown about the Neck, without Form or Decency — A tumbled, discoloured Mob, or Night Cap, half on, and half off, with the frowsy Hair, hanging in sweaty Ringlets, staring like Medusa with her Serpents — Shrugging up her Petticoats, that are sweeping the Ground, and scarce ty'd on, — Hands unwashed — Teeth furr'd — and Eyes crusted: —

But I beg your Pardon, I'll go no farther with this sluttish Picture, which I am afraid has already turned your Stomach. If the Copy, and but an Imperfect one it is, be so shocking to us, what think you must the Original be to the poor Wretch her Husband, who, perhaps, for some Hours every Day in the Week, has the comfortable Sight and Odour of this Tatterdemalion?

God help his Stomach! This is the real Portrait of many married Women, and the piteous Case of many a poor Soul of a Husband; unless when happily some Stranger is expected, then Madam takes care to appear clean, and thereby convinces her Husband, she is more anxious to please a Stranger than the Man who has chosen her as his Companion for Life.

A constant Care and Study to preserve the Economy and Sweetness of Dress and Person, must be of great Service to support Love and Esteem in Wedlock .

I don't hereby intend or mean Foppery or Finery, but that Neatness and Cleanliness, which neither is nor ought to be ashamed of seeing or being seen by any Body .

. . .

EACH Person should be so duly attentive to their respective Province of Management, as to conduct it with the utmost Prudence and Discretion in their Power.

. . .

THAT Part of Management which belongs to the preserving our Interest, or improving our Fortune, usually falls, and very properly, on the Man. And 'tis unquestionably incumbent on him, if he be a Man of Estate, and independent of any Business, to regulate his Equipage, his private and family Expenses, according to the Income of his Fortune; and 'tis certainly a Point of Prudence not to live quite up to that; but to lay up a Fund, to which he may have recourse in any of those adverse Occurrences to which even the most exalted Stations are liable.

. . .

NO ridiculous Vanity or foolish Ambition

should suffer the Husband or Wife, in their Dress, Furniture, or whole Way of Life, to exceed their Income or Fortune.

THEIR Appearance and Expenses, should neither degenerate into Sordidness, nor run into wild Extravagance.

THAT particular Part of Management called House-wifery, belongs to the Woman, and we shall comprise it under these three Divisions.

A PRUDENT FRUGALITY,

NEATNESS, AND A HARMONIOUS ECONOMY

. . .

HOWEVER unskillfully this Argument may have been handled by me, and of how little Advantage soever my weak Attempts may have been to serve it; the Truth of the following Propositions remains in Force .

FIRST. That unhappy Matches are often occasioned by meer mercenary Views, in one or both of the parties: Or by the head-strong Motives of ill-conducted Passion .

SECONDLY, That by a prudent and judicious Proceeding in our Addresses to a Young Lady of a good natural Temper, we may lay a very good Foundation for making her an agreeable Companion, a steady Friend , and a good Wife.

AND Thirdly: That after Marriage, by continuing in the Road of Prudence and Judgment, we may make the nuptial State as happy as we can promise our selves from any other .

To conclude, Sir, whenever I am inclined for a matrimonial voyage, I shall endeavour thus to steer my Course, and if I cannot gain the Port by this Manner of Courtship and Conduct, I will rest contented with my present Condition.

IF, on the other Hand, I should there by gain the Inclinations and Consent of a Lady, I shall endeavour to support my Happiness in some such Manner as I have herein intimated.

I am, & c.

Wally, Wally...The Beggar's Opera

In Firebrand, Polly announces her favorite music is found in the production of *The Beggars Opera*.

Polly is also the name of a character in *The Beggars Opera*.

The following describes an Opera, this being the second part of the Beggars Opera (1729).

Some suggest that Mr. Gay, a student of Handel who dominated the opera scene, started working on the opera in 1727.

In its first season, this opera ran 32 nights, with over sixty performances. On February 1, 1728, The Daily Journal reported *"No theatrical performance for many years has met with so much applause."*

In England, King George II overturned the Puritan decree to outlaw all theatrical performances (1642) where "actors were to be punished as rogues".

The King who loved to have a fun party issued patents to two companies which would later become "Drury Lane" and "Covent Gardens", theaters in London, England.

During this Restoration period, playwrites would cater to King George's thirst for wit, establishing a new genre of theatrical works: "Comedy of Manners".

These plays would present human flaws and weakness presented in a witty and satirical manner, while possibly affirming King George's ultimate superiority as the monarch who would never deign to make the foolish choices enacted by the characters on stage.

This was to be the first work demonstrating political satire and some critics felt each character represented a real-life political message.

This opera opened the door for other political messages to be hidden inside a storyline.

It was this political satire that led to the Licensing Act of 1737. This inspired Henry Fielding to begin political drama works... until the Licensing Act discouraged political messages as well as the favorable portrayal of criminals, as this would appeal to lower classes of society and make opera accessible to the common man, showing that the public's taste was declining.

This would open the door to the movement of "Sentimentalism", which was a "tragi-comedy" work which was comedic yet absurdly dramatic.

The characters in the Beggar's Opera were foolish. The characters in a typical sentimental work would make an ideal choice to demonstrate that good triumphs over evil. Many writers disapproved of the sentimental movement, which remained popular to the late 1700's. . .

Summary of *the Beggar's Opera*: Storyline

The Beggars Opera is about a thief-catcher, Mr. Peachum, who learns his daughter, Polly, has married Macheath, a highwayman, a man who robs travelers at gunpoint.

Polly's parents decide the bounty for Macheath would pay well and decide to kill him. Eventually, Macheath is placed in Newgate prison where the warden's daughter, Lucy Lockit, falls in love with him and he proposes to her... until Polly shows up clarifying that she is already his wife. Polly works with Lucy to free Macheath while Lucy plans to poison Polly, but Polly is too clever and avoids the poisoned cup.

Meanwhile, Macheath is recaptured and sent to the gallows to die, so both Polly and Lucy plead with their fathers to save Macheath. Macheath is released and acknowledges that Polly was his true wife all along.

This was an opera intended to provide the audience with a "happily ever after" ending.

P O L L Y:

10
z

A N

O P E R A.

BEING THE

SECOND PART

OF THE

BEGGAR's OPERA.

Written by Mr. *G A T.*

Rarò antecedentem fcelefum
Deferuit pede pœna claudo. Hor.

L O N D O N:
Printed for T. THOMSON, and fold by the Book-
fellers of *London* and *Weftminfter.* 1729.
[*Price One Shilling and Sixpence.*]

Polly. Why have I a heart so constant? cruel love!

A I R VII. O Waly, Waly, up the bank.

Farewell, farewell, all hope of bliss!
For Polly *always must be thine.*
Shall then my heart be never his,
Which never can again be mine?
O Love, you play a cruel part,
Thy shaft still festers in the wound;
You should reward a constant heart,
Since 'tis, alas, so seldom found!

and she is gone off with him. You must give over all thoughts of him, for he is a very Devil to our Sex; not a Woman of the greatest Vivacity shifts her Inclinations half so fast as he can. Besides, he would disown you; for, like an Upstart, he hates an old Acquaintance. I am sorry to see those Tears, Child, but I love you too well to flatter you.

Polly. Why have I a Heart so constant? cruel Love!

A I R VII.   O waly, waly, up the Bank.

> *Farewel, farewel, all Hope of Bliss,*
>   *For* Polly *always must be thine:*
> *Shall then my Heart be never his,*
>   *Which never can again be mine?*
> *O Love, you play a cruel Part,*
>   *Thy Shaft still festers in the Wound,*
> *You should reward a constant Heart,*
>   *Since 'tis alas! so seldom found.*

Trap. I tell you once again, Miss *Polly,* you must think no more of him. You are like a Child who is crying after a Butterfly, that is hopping and fluttering upon every Flower in the Field; there is not a Woman that comes in his Way but he must have a Taste of; besides, there is no catching him. But, my dear Girl, I hope you took Care, at your leaving *England,* to bring off wherewithal to support you.

Polly. Since he is lost, I am insensible of every other Misfortune. I brought, indeed, a Sum of Money with me, but my Chest was broke open at Sea, and I am now a wretched Vagabond, expos'd to Hunger and Want, unless Charity relieve me.

Trap. Poor Child! Your Father and I have had great Dealings together, and I shall be grateful to his Memory. I will look upon you as my Daughter; you shall be with me.

Polly. As soon as I can have Remittances from *England,* I shall be able to acknowledge your Goodness. I have still Five Hundred Pounds there, which will be return'd to me upon Demand; but I had rather undertake an honest Service, that might afford me a Maintenance, than be burthensom to my Friends.

Image 1 Act I, Air Vii & corresponding music for Air 7

DESCENDANTS

How do the characters in Firebrand relate to the characters in Edges? Below is a simple diagram showing the ancestors:

Man 1776	Woman 1776		Descendant 2030's
Button Gwinette	Polly Mulhooin	→	Bjorn Esterday, Investigative Reporter
Bryce Aiden Tyler	Jane Hargreaves	→	Sarah Paradise, Teacher
Billy Dawes	Silversmith	→	Earth Farmer Community

		→	Sammy Scribe, Editor of Daily Memo Newspaper in Courtly City
Magistrate Karl Pinkney	Eliza Lucas		
Irish Sailor Patrick Scriobhai	Susanna Wright	→	Mrs. Libris, Courtly City librarian
Witherspoon	Grand Estate Cook	→	Queenie Courtly, Originally from AromaX and married to Jack Courtly, ruling couple of Courtly City.
Clergy Pastor at the Church	Polly's Mother	→	No descendants... they simply married and lived happily ever after together...
TallMan		→	Guard Gene who gets promoted to Detective Ivan Emilio Gene

15 Vocabulary

In the early 1770s, before the colonies united into the United States of America, some words and terms were used, which may be explained in this section.

Absurd: Foolish, silly.

Accessible: Easy to reach.

Decline: To say "no." To refuse. Or to bend

Define: To describe the meaning of a word, or what an object does or looks like.

Discourage: To oppose. To give up hope.

Inspired: Brilliant, outstanding, as if done by divine direction.

Licensing: The government gives a person or group special permission to do something.

Political: A person or group that controls or wants to control the government.

Portray/ portrayal: To describe, to represent. To act on stage.

Sentimental: Showing affectionate gentle, feelings, as in a play onstage.

Satire: A literary genre. A style of writing in which human foolishness is laughed at, often with sarcasm.

ABOUT Wynter Sommers

Wynter Sommers is the pseudonym for an American writing team, which harnesses multiple skills in technology, research, history and education. Formally trained with a PhD in Education, Wynter Sommers blends academic classroom experience, with corporate sophistication, and a passion for developing more effective student insights through engaging storytelling.

Wynter Sommers has a heart to inspire creativity and develop critical thinking skills, all to encourage readers to make wise choices in life.

Wynter Sommers takes each story and weaves the plot with classic gripping elements, which endure throughout repeated readings, revealing new meanings each time the story is explored. The small choices a reader makes in real life could have a lasting effect in future generations. This set of stories shows the origin of not just Bjorn Esterday and Sarah Paradise, but of their ancestors and the sort of world which was established, which unfolded in each generation until Bjorn and Sarah met.

It is rewarding to learn of heartfelt, thought provoking conversations taking place globally about the characters of these books. Should the reader be presented with extraordinary circumstances, it is the sincerest wish that they act with honor, truth and integrity to overcome obstacles in real life whilst the reader hones skills of self-reliance and collaborative teamwork despite barriers outside of the reader's control. Wynter Sommers hopes you enjoy the other *Bjorn Esterday Was not Born Yesterday* stories in this series.

www.ingramcontent.com/pod-product-compliance
Lightning Source LLC
Chambersburg PA
CBHW030036030726
47500CB00001B/128